For my parents, my siblings and their spouses, and
Samantha, Sebastian, Jeremy and Alexander.   —*David Seow*

For Father, with whom all things are possible.
And for the child in all us.   —*L.K. Tay-Audouard*

Cultural Background

The Chinese classic *Journey to the West,* or *Monkey King* as it is
popularly known, was written by Wu Ch'eng-en (1500-1582) and
has been a favorite story for generations of Chinese around the
world. Inspired by the life of the famous monk, Xuan Zang, who
journeyed to India in search of holy Buddhist scriptures, Wu
Ch'eng-en crafted an amazing, wondrous tale with elements of
Chinese legends and folktales along with aspects of Buddhist and
Taoist mythology.

Published by Tuttle Publishing,
an imprint of Periplus Editions (HK) Ltd,
with editorial offices at 153 Milk Street,
Boston, Massachusetts 02109 and 130 Joo
Seng Road #06-01, Singapore 368357

LCC Card No: 2004110836
ISBN 0-8048-3517-9
First printing, 2005
Printed in Singapore
09 08 07 06 05 04
6   5   4   3   2   1

Distributed by:

North America, Latin America & Europe
Tuttle Publishing
364 Innovation Drive, North Clarendon
VT 05759-9436, USA
Tel: (802) 773 8930, Fax: (802) 773 6993
Email: info@tuttlepublishing.com
Website: www.tuttlepublishing.com

Asia Pacific
Berkeley Books Pte Ltd
130 Joo Seng Road #06-01
Singapore 368357
Tel: (65) 6280 1330, Fax: (65) 6280 6290
Email: inquiries@periplus.com.sg
Website: www.periplus.com

Japan
Tuttle Publishing
Yaekari Building, 3F
5-4-12 Osaki, Shinagawa-ku
Tokyo 141-0032
Tel: (03) 5437 0171, Fax: (03) 5437 0755
Email: tuttle-sales@gol.com

MONKEY

The Classic Chinese Adventure Tale

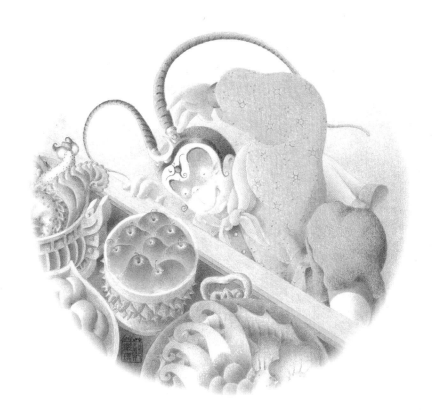

by **David Seow**

illustrations by **L.K. Tay-Audouard**

TUTTLE PUBLISHING
Boston • Rutland, Vermont • Tokyo

Long ago, the country of China was in great disorder. The people were filled with anger, hatred, jealousy, and greed.

The Jade Emperor, the ruler of the Heavens, asked his gods and goddesses, "What shall I do? Should I destroy them all with a great bolt of lightning?"

Guan Yin, the Goddess of Mercy, replied, "Your Majesty, the people can be helped. Lord Buddha has written scriptures that show the way to peace, love, kindness, and harmony. These scriptures are somewhere in India. If we can find them and bring them back to China, they will show the people how to behave."

The Jade Emperor agreed. He commanded Guan Yin to find him someone brave and noble enough to face the many dangers the search for the scriptures would require.

After years of searching, Guan Yin found Xuan Zang, a monk with a pure and noble heart, in a tiny village in the north of China. She told Xuan Zang about the Jade Emperor's orders and warned him, "Finding the scriptures will not be easy—you will cross treacherous lands filled with bandits, demons, ogres, and terrible beasts. Some people will try to stop you, because they want the world to stay in turmoil. But if you go, you will not go without friends."

Xuan Zang replied, "I've devoted my life to bringing peace and knowledge to mankind. I accept the challenge!"

Guan Yin gave Xuan Zang a priest's silk robe and a magnificent white horse. She named him Tripitaka—the Great Scripture Seeker—and wished him a safe journey. And so his adventures began....

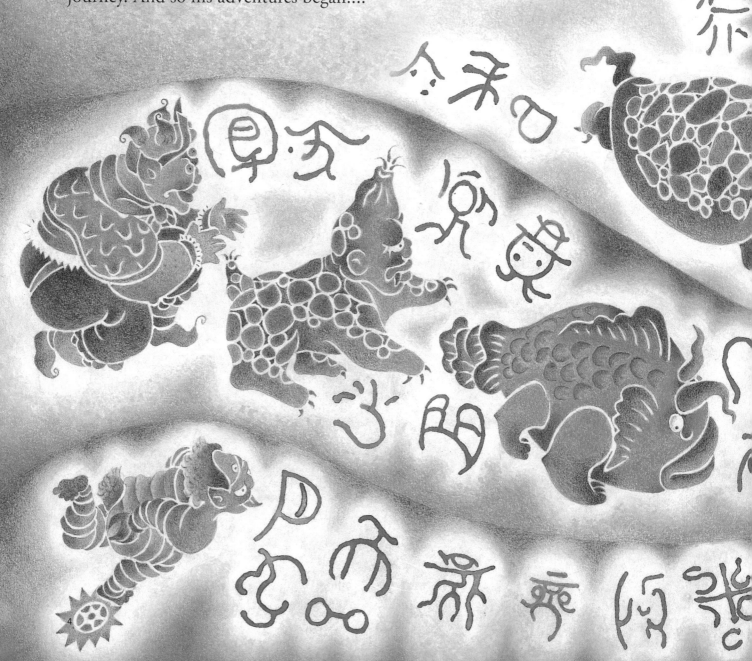

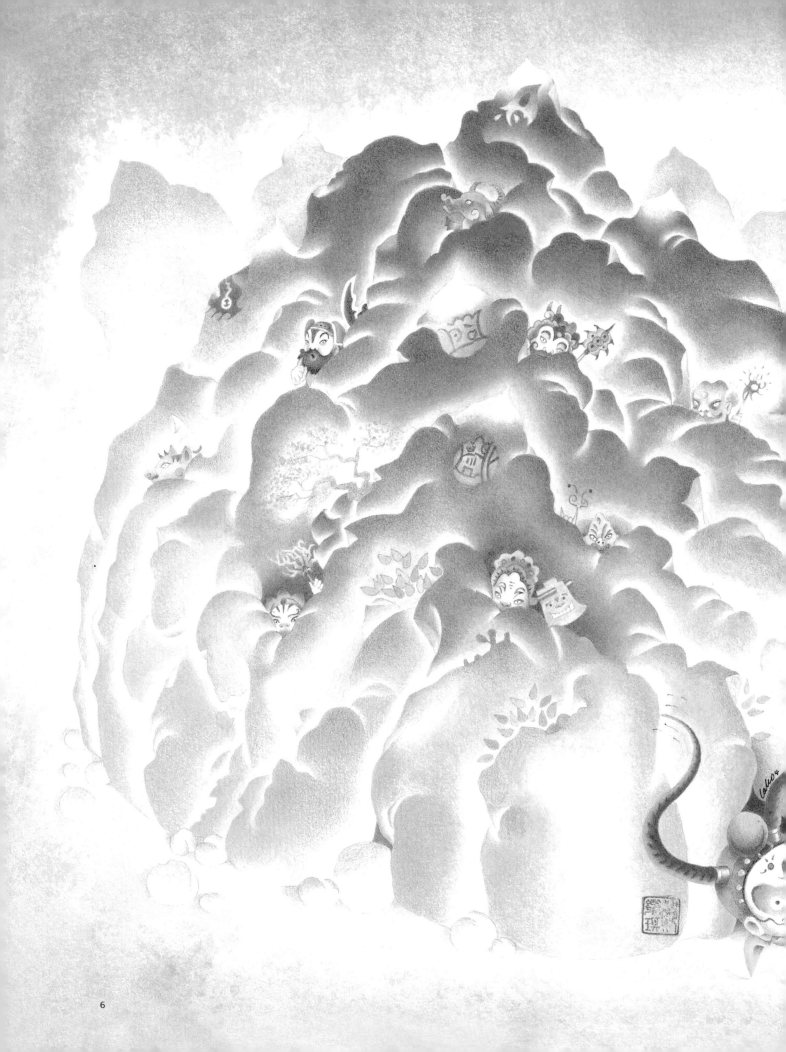

After thirty days of traveling toward India, Tripitaka approached the Five Elements Mountain, where ugly hunchbacked ogres and strange animals lay in wait for travelers. The road got rough, and the fields looked overgrown and abandoned. Gathering his courage, Tripitaka rode into the forest at the base of the mountain. CR—EAK! GRR! GRR! UNN—UNNN! Terrible sounds echoed throughout the dark forest. Cold winds whistled, and the trees swayed overhead, their branches reaching out like bony hands.

"Ha ha ha!" a shrill laugh echoed eerily in the distance. Tripitaka peered timidly into the darkness, looking for the source of the voice. His horse shook with fear.

"Hee hee hee!" now louder and sounding much closer.

Tripitaka calmed his horse and dismounted. Suddenly, out of nowhere, something grabbed his foot!

"Ahh!" Looking down, he saw a furry hand clasped around his ankle, and a monkey's face with twinkling eyes staring back at him.

"Did you make those noises?" Tripitaka demanded.

"Hee Hee Hee! Yes, I did!" the monkey laughed as he let go of Tripitaka's ankle.

"You gave me quite a scare! Who are you, and why do you live on this terrifying mountain?"

"I am Monkey, King of the Mountain of Flowers and Fruit, Great Sage Equal to Heaven, with fantastic powers of transformation! I was cast out of Heaven five hundred years ago for wrecking the Jade Emperor's heavenly banquet. I have been kept a prisoner under this mountain ever since," explained Monkey.

Tripitaka was puzzled. "That seems like such a harsh punishment!"

Monkey's eyes sparkled with mischief. "I'm sure the Jade Emperor would have forgiven me for ruining the banquet—if I had stopped there." Monkey wriggled in excitement. "I ate the tastiest food that day—wings of flying fish,

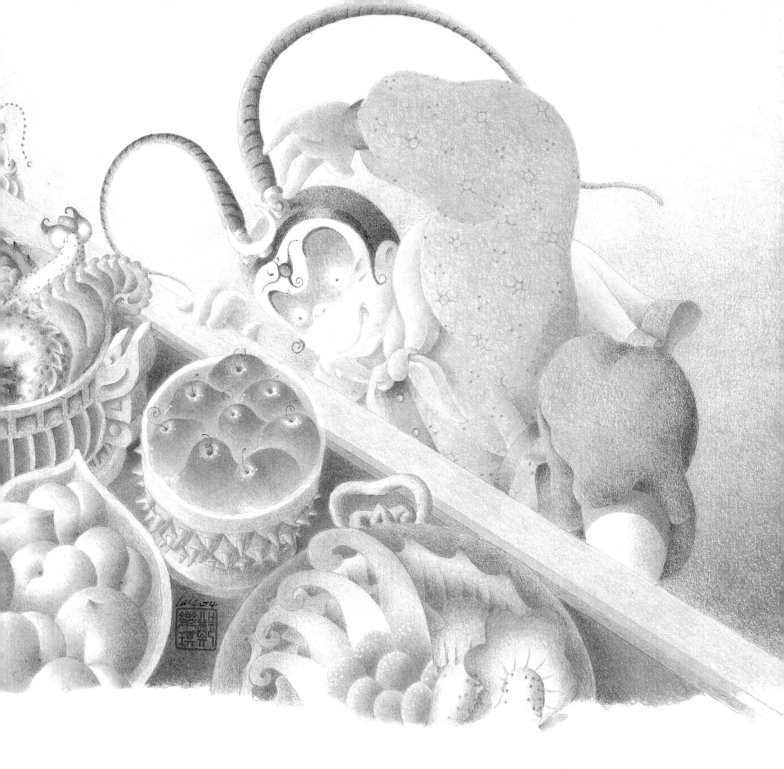

tail of Fujian dragon, rainbow eggs of jeweled carp, and more! But most delicious of all was the Elixir of Immortality. This belongs to the Jade Emperor and only he can drink this elixir. First I took a sip—Ah, it was heavenly! I couldn't stop myself, and I gulped it all down. The Jade Emperor was so angry that he imprisoned me here until I redeem myself by helping the Great Scripture Seeker."

"But I am the Great Scripture Seeker!" Tripitaka said, shocked. Monkey laughed gleefuly. "What luck! At last! You have the power to release me!"

Tripitaka recalled Guan Yin's words—perhaps Monkey could help him. He looked skyward and said, "If Monkey is truly to join my quest, release him!"

The mountain crumbled into ash and blew away in the wind. Monkey shook off five hundred years of dust and dirt.

"Do you really have magical powers?" asked Tripitaka, settling himself on a large rock.

Monkey's face lit up. "I can transform myself in one thousand and one ways. I can turn one of my hairs into ten thousand small monkeys! And I can hop onto clouds and circle the world three times in the blink of an eye!"

Before Tripitaka could blink, Monkey leapt onto a cloud and disappeared. An instant later, he reappeared overhead in the branches of a large tree. Then he vanished again—and reappeared sitting on the rock next to Tripitaka. Monkey's speed and agility were beyond belief! Tripitaka laughed in delight.

Suddenly, the rocks they were both sitting on began to shake. They jumped off just in time—and watched in horror as two giant ogres, one green, one blue, rose from the ground, towering over them. What they'd thought were rocks had actually been the ogres' heads!

"Lunch!" shouted the green ogre. "Mine!" shouted the blue ogre. Pushing and shoving, both scrambled to be the first to grab Tripitaka.

"Leave my Master alone!" ordered Monkey, but the ogres ignored him. Ogres are not particularly smart, so Monkey decided to trick them. He vanished, then reappeared behind them, and gave each of them a powerful slap. The ogres hadn't seen Monkey move, so the green ogre thought the blue ogre had hit him, and the blue ogre thought the green ogre had hit him. They slapped each other back and forth with such strength and speed that they quickly reduced each other to puddles of goo.

Tripitaka heaved a big sigh of relief. Without warning, Monkey flung a huge staff that whizzed just past Tripitaka's shoulder.

"What—?" Tripitaka started to ask angrily, but as he turned, he saw that the staff had plunged straight into the heart of a tiger poised to pounce. "You saved me again! Thank you!" Tripitaka cried in relief.

Leaving the dangers of the
Five Elements Mountain behind,
they entered the Great Bamboo Forest.
Suddenly a loud scream pierced the air.
"Aah ... Help!" a girl cried out as she ran toward
Tripitaka for safety from a hideous pig-like creature chasing her.

"Give Pigsy your buns. I want your red bean buns!" Pigsy shouted, as he
greedily took the buns from the pretty girl's basket. Pigsy quickly turned and
raced deeper into the forest when he saw Monkey rushing toward him.

"Prepare to meet your doom!" shouted Monkey at the start of a fierce battle that
left all the trees in the forest shaking wildly. Pigsy fought hard blocking Monkey's
powerful blows thousands of times—but his rake was no match for Monkey's
magical staff, and exhausted he dropped his rake in defeat. "Ha! Now I can
destroy you and be on my way with the Great Scripture Seeker," Monkey cried.

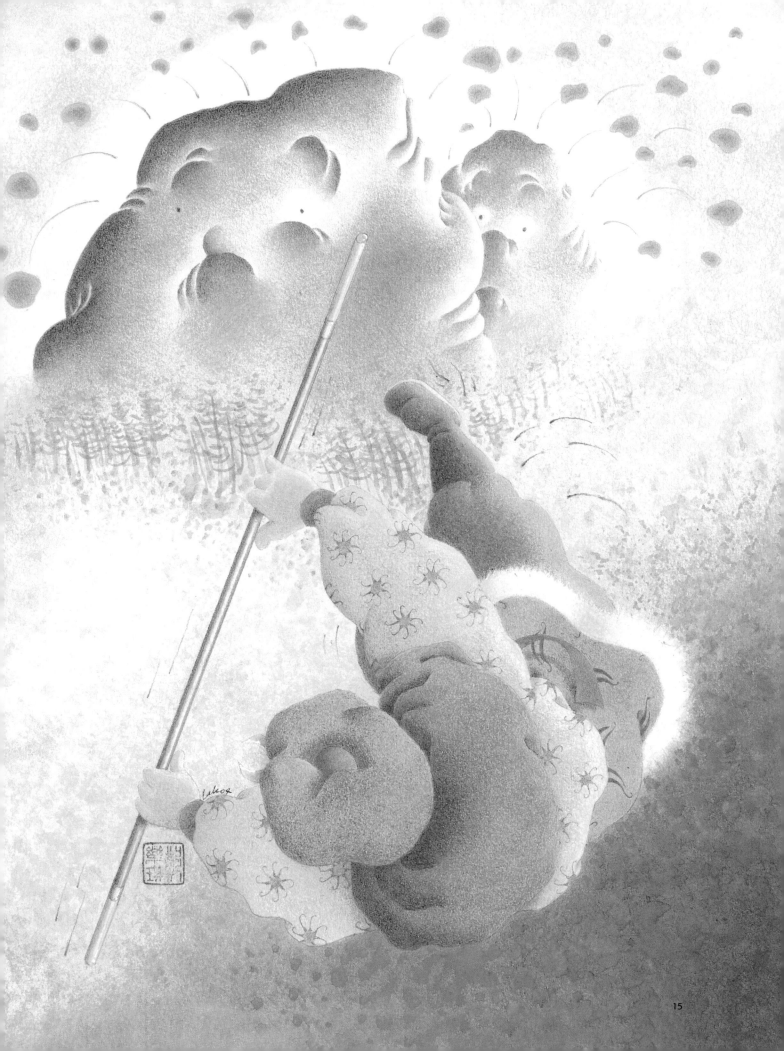

"The Scripture Seeker?" Pigsy squealed in surprise. "You must take me to him! My only hope is to help him!"

Monkey chuckled. "You want to join the Scripture Seeker, too?"

Pigsy scowled. "I wasn't always like this, you know. I used to be Keeper of the Heavenly Gardens—a playground for the Jade Empress. But I was unable to resist the Empress's beauty, and one day I declared my love for her! The Jade Emperor was furious. He turned me into an ugly pig-like creature and banished me. I can only leave this vast forest if the Great Scripture Seeker lets me help him."

"Let me take you to my Master. He will decide if you can join us," Monkey said.

Tripitaka listened carefully to Pigsy's story. He knew Pigsy could help him on his journey, and so the three traveled onward together.

After many days of travel they came to the Great Sandy Bottom River, which was so wide and murky that they couldn't see the other side.

Pigsy was shaking in terror. "I've heard that a horrible monster lives in this raging river and destroys everything in its path! How will we cross safely?"

"All I have to do is leap onto a cloud!" boasted Monkey, puffing out his furry chest with pride.

"But what about us?" asked Pigsy. "Can you turn into a boat and take us across?"

"No, I can only turn myself into living things ..." Before Monkey could fully explain, Pigsy interrupted and snorted, "Well, that's not very helpful, is it? I thought you were the Great Sage Equal to Heaven!"

"I am!" said Monkey angrily. "Maybe you can float across the river on your fat stomach! Ha! Ha! Ha!" he roared.

Pigsy and Monkey were so busy arguing that they didn't notice misty shadows gathering behind them and a giant monster—with fiery amber eyes and golden spiky hair—rising slowly. With one quick swipe, the monster snatched Tripitaka's white horse and plunged beneath the dark surface of the water.

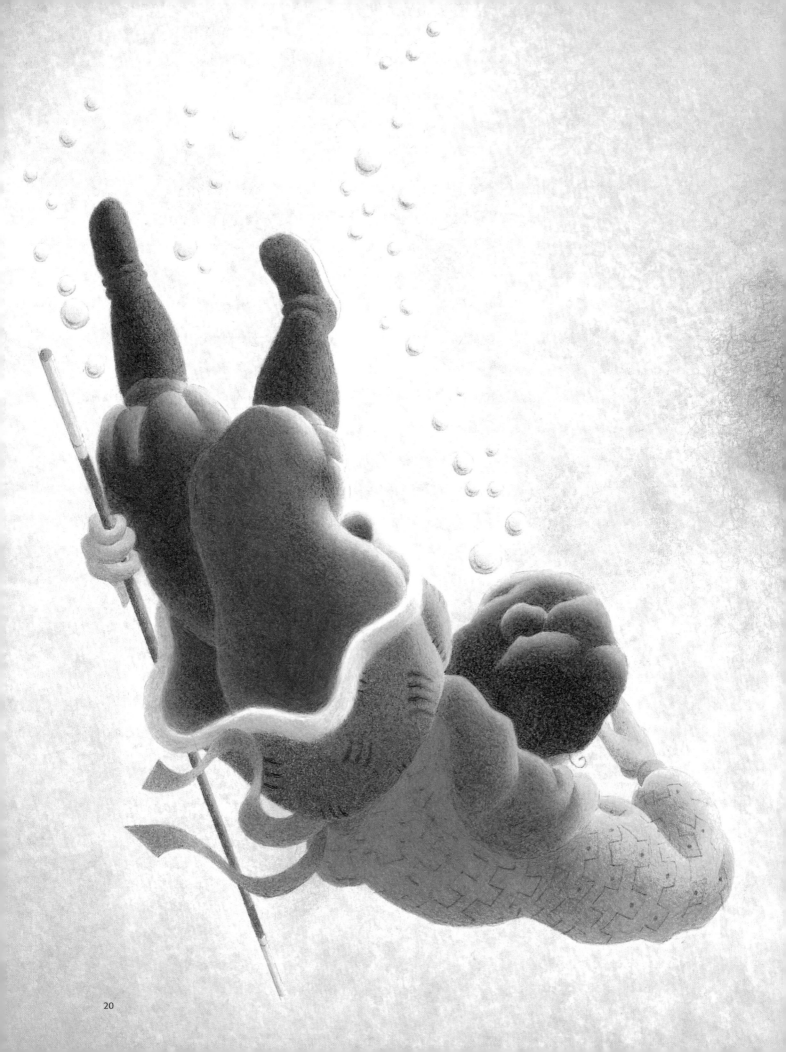

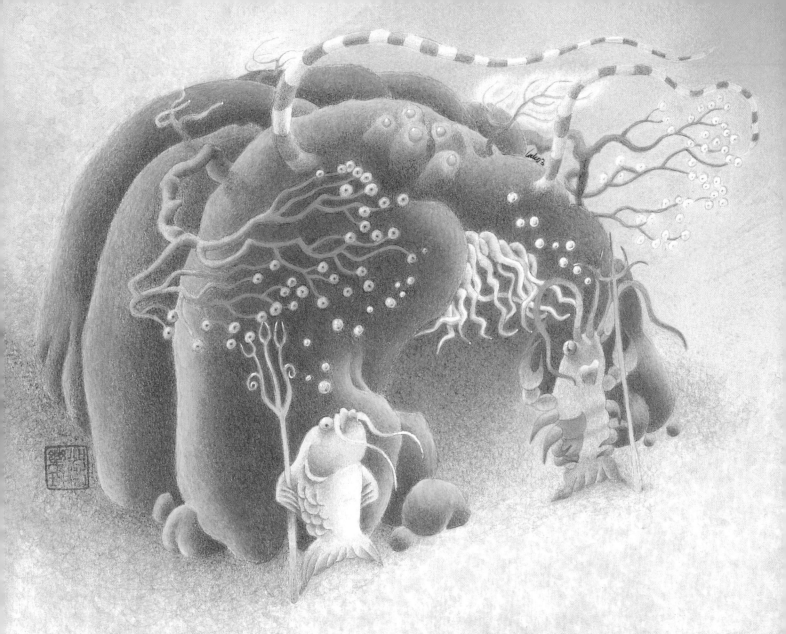

The monster swam down toward a large underwater cave guarded by
fierce fish and lobster sentries. Monkey dived into the river to give chase.

"Return the horse or suffer the consequences!" Monkey demanded.

Roaring with laughter, the monster sent one thousand fish and lobster
soldiers to capture Monkey. Monkey plucked a hair from the top of his head
and turned it into ten thousand small monkeys—who quickly defeated
the attackers.

"I guess I'll have to destroy Monkey myself!" cried the monster, picking up
a large sword, and rushing out of his cave. He looked all around, but couldn't
find Monkey. "Ha! The coward has fled," the monster said triumphantly.
But Monkey had changed himself into a water beetle with very sharp pincers!
He jumped on the monster's back and pinched as hard as he could. With a
painful cry, the monster shot out of the water and landed on the riverbank.

Monkey changed back into himself, he and Pigsy fought the river monster for hours. Their ferocious combat could be heard for miles around. They were so busy fighting that they didn't see a giant eagle swooping down toward Tripitaka. The eagle caught Tripitaka in its strong talons and carried him high into the air, flying away over the mountaintops.

"Oh no! Look the eagle has snatched our Master, the Great Scripture Seeker!" shouted Pigsy.

The river monster abruptly stopped his attack. Monkey and Pigsy eyed him suspiciously, still clutching their weapons.

"You're traveling with the Great Scripture Seeker?" the monster asked excitedly. Monkey nodded. "Please, let me help!" the monster begged.

23

"My name is Sandy and I need to redeem myself in the eyes of the Jade Emperor."

Stunned, Monkey and Pigsy lowered their weapons, waiting for an explanation.

"I was once the Jade Emperor's favorite chef. When I had a chance I entertained my kitchen staff by balancing plates, cups and bowls. One day, the Jade Emperor caught me! He tried to rescue his favorite cup, but I lost my balance, and—Clink! Clank! Crash!—everything came tumbling down, smashing into thousands of pieces. The Jade Emperor was so angry that he turned me into a monster and banished me to the Great Sandy Bottom River —until I could help the Great Scripture Seeker."

Monkey and Pigsy decided to bring Sandy along. Monkey transformed himself into a giant falcon. Pigsy and Sandy hopped on his back, and they chased the giant eagle over the mountain ridges into a large ravine, where they were attacked by a flock of savage eagles. Fighting furiously on all sides, Monkey, Pigsy, and Sandy were just able to drive the eagles away.

They tracked the giant eagle to a large cave on the side of a rocky mountain. Monkey changed back into himself, and the three entered the cave together. It was littered with feathers, scaly claws, crushed bones and skulls, and smelled of blood and death.

Gathering their courage, they called out, "Master, where are you?" Their voices rang through the cave. "Master!"

"I'm here, in this basket full of giant boulders," Tripitaka called back from above. "Quick, help me get out before the eagle comes back!"

They had almost reached Tripitaka when a large, dark shadow loomed above them ...

the giant eagle had returned! It grabbed Pigsy and Sandy and flung them into the basket.

Hoping to distract the giant eagle so that the others could escape, Monkey turned himself into a large, plump, tasty-looking bird and flew away. The giant eagle gave chase.

Sandy explained his presence to Tripitaka. "In Heaven, I had the power to turn objects into anything I desired. Maybe now that I've come to help you, that power will be restored! Let's see if I can turn this basket into something we can easily break."

Sandy snapped his fingers and the basket magically changed into a fragile porcelain bowl. But the basket had not been full of boulders—it was the eagle's nest and full of giant eagle eggs!

Before they could escape the baby eagles hatched from their shells and began chirping loudly.

The giant eagle stopped chasing Monkey and hurried back to the hatchlings. Pigsy hit the bowl with all his might. Whack! Porcelain shards flew everywhere. One piece pierced the giant eagle's heart, killing it instantly.

29

They were still in danger—angry hatchlings out for revenge loomed all around. Fighting together, they made quick work of the hatchlings. Then turning again into a falcon, Tripitaka, Pigsy, and Sandy flew on Monkey's back to a safe place for a rest.

That evening Sandy cooked a feast fit for an emperor, using his magic to turn pebbles into grapes, twigs into chopsticks and knives, and leaves into plates. Sandy even made a special dish out of roast hatchlings! As they started eating, each gave his own version of the exciting events of the day.

"I did an amazing job of rescuing Master," said Sandy.

"You? What about me? I smashed the nest!" replied Pigsy.

"But you wouldn't have been able to break it if I hadn't turned it into porcelain!" countered Sandy.

"Hey, what about me?" said Monkey. "I lured the giant eagle away. I am the real hero today!"

Tripitaka grew tired of their squabbling. "Enough!" he said. "You all helped rescue me—it took all of you to beat that giant eagle. If we're going to find Lord Buddha's scriptures, we've got to keep working together. Can I count on you?"

Monkey, Pigsy, and Sandy muttered and glanced at each other. It seemed like a tall order.

"We can't promise that we won't fight, but we'll try not to do it so often!" vowed Monkey.

"We all really want to find the scriptures and restore peace to China," Sandy said.

"And we all want to impress the Jade Emperor and make up for our bad behavior," Pigsy added.

The three disciples pledged to work together to protect Tripitaka on his long journey to India and back.

After a good night's rest, Monkey, Pigsy, Sandy, and Tripitaka continued onward toward India. They would face many incredible adventures along the way—but that is another story....